BLOOD MAGICK

THE ORDER OF FATE

MOON RIVER MATES
BOOK ONE

TAVITA LANE

Take back your power and show them who you are.

READING ORDER

Magick Thief (The Order of Fate Book One)
Blood Magick (Moon River Mates)
Night Magick (The Order of Fate Book Two)
Wolf Magick (Moon River Mates book Two)

CHAPTER 1
CASSIE

Eating dirt was not on Cassie's agenda for the day. But it seemed like that was all she was doing lately.

"You're the one that wanted to learn how to fight with your hands versus your magick," a deep voice boomed over her.

Cassie dug her hands into the dirt and pushed herself to her feet. She glared at the half dressed man standing in front of her with his hands wrapped in white hand wraps hanging at his side.

"I know, but you didn't have to hit so hard," Cassie said.

He sighed. "I'm sorry, are you okay?" He stepped towards her and she took a wide swing, catching his jaw.

She smirked and stepped back, but a part of her knew he saw it coming. Carik was just giving her a hit to make her feel better. That made her more angry than before.

"You got me," he said, putting his hands up. "What do you say we take a break?"

"A break?" Cassie put her hands on her hips and watched him. Going easy on her wasn't really his style. *What is he up to?*

"I'm tired and we've been fighting all morning," Carik said, cocking an eyebrow. "Aren't you tired?"

"No," she lied. The truth was she was exhausted. Ever since Cassie had stolen the weird book of the future, she'd been seeing it non stop. That was one of the perks of stealing something like that. Cody warned her before he got all dead and all that the book would change her, but no one told her she'd become the book. At least not until it was too late.

"I still have to figure out what we need to do. You know, to save the future?" Cassie sat on the grass and pulled at the hand wraps. Her hand stung with the impact she'd given Carik, but she didn't let on. The last thing she wanted was him to know she needed anything or that she was in any kind of pain.

He watched her, but didn't move to comfort her or anything. She was relieved at that. When Carik and her first met, he was convinced he was in love with her, but fortunately her attitude had come through and let him know how bad that idea was for him and for her.

"I'm going in. You shouldn't stay out here too long. There are things that might still be after you, you know."

"I'm a Witch, I can take care of myself," Cassie snapped. She held his gaze and he sucked in a breath before turning and walking back to the house. She pulled the hand wraps off and threw them at the dirt. This was what her life had become. A Witch with almost no family and everything she'd known turned upside down.

Her father wasn't her father and her mother, well she wasn't who she thought she was either. At least she still had her sister. Lark was the only constant she had and fortunately she'd somehow escaped death.

So much family drama.

Now they were the only ones that could keep the Vampires and Demons from destroying everything, but Cassie still had no idea where to start.

"Sitting on the job, little Witch?" A familiar voice said from behind her.

Cassie sighed but didn't turn towards him.

"What? You go off on your own with my lovely brother for a while and think you're better than everyone here?" He walked past her and leaned on the wall of the house next to her.

"What do you want, Kierin?" Cassie snapped.

"Oh come on, I'm just here to help, same as Carik," Kierin said with a smile. "That's why you're here, right?"

Cassie turned to him and shook her head. "I'm here because I need to learn more about how this power works," She said, letting her hands fall at her side. "As I recall, you're not the one connected to the book."

"Ouch, you didn't have to remind me how well connected you are to my brother," he said, mocking her. "Maybe you should have stuck around the first time instead of running off to save the world."

"I saved my sister," she said through gritted teeth.

He stepped closer and kept his eyes on her. "Did you? As I recall she died and then came back to life. Weird, right?"

"Stay out of my life, Kierin."

"Or what, little Witch?" He stepped closer, his dark eyes pinning her down.

Cassie licked her lips, trying to think of a comeback, but nothing would come out. A throat cleared behind her and Kierin's smile broadened.

"Don't worry, little brother. We were just talking," he said before sliding past Cassie and walking away.

Carik

. . .

"Wʜᴀᴛ ᴛʜᴇ ʜᴇʟʟ ᴡᴀꜱ ᴛʜᴀᴛ?" Carick felt his face heating with anger, but tried to keep it under wraps.

"Come on Carik, it's not like we're a thing. I don't need you to come after every man I talk to," Cassie snapped.

She was right. They weren't in a relationship anymore. It almost hurt him more to think about it than when he was forced to say it. Things here weren't safe for her and they were only going to get worse.

"Still, you don't want to have a thing with a wolf and definitely not that one," he growled. He wasn't going to let it go. not when it came to Kerian. She deserved better than his brother.

"Who said I was interested in having a thing?" Cassie crossed her arms and stared at him.

He just grumbled and turned back towards the house. Carik could feel her walking behind him, but he didn't look back. They both were training hard for whatever this future was they both saw. He wasn't going to make it weirder if he could help it. Not that having a thing with her and then breaking it off didn't make it weird already.

"I'm going to take a nap. You can figure out whatever this is without me," Cassie snapped as they both walked into the house. He glanced back at her before heading towards the living room and she swung around the corner and headed upstairs.

This is the right choice.

"Keep telling yourself that," Kieran said from the couch. He was slouching with a beer in his hand, something locally brewed.

Carik crossed his arms and stared at him for a moment.

"What? I can see it all over your face."

"Stay away from Cassie. She has bigger things to think about than you," Carik said without moving.

Kieran smiled and took a drink of his beer. "She's her own woman. She can tell me when or if she wants me to leave her alone."

"Would you?"

"Would I what?" He said while watching Carik.

"Leave her alone?"

Kieran kept his eyes on Carik and smiled. Carik didn't have to ask. He knew his brother. He'd do what he wanted and Cassie would get caught up in his games if she wasn't careful.

Realizing he wasn't going to get anywhere with him, Carik walked past him and walked into the garage. He closed the door behind him and leaned against the wall. Then he remembered.

The way she looked against his work bench when he was kissing her. His hands roaming up her body. This was the worst place for him to be. It reminded him too much of the short time they'd been together and he couldn't go back there, not if he was planning on keeping them both alive.

He ran his hand through his hair and sighed, this was torture and he'd done it to himself.

CHAPTER 2

CASSIE

She walked into the room she'd taken as her own and shut the door behind her. A part of her hoped they heard how hard the door slammed and knew she was pissed. How could they keep telling her what she was supposed to do? Carik thought he knew what was best for her, but he wasn't the one with this power, this curse.

Cassie didn't want to see the future. Sure it sounded good when it was a good future, but the things she'd seen, the people that were going to die, it was too much for anyone. That was why there was supposed to be a Wolf companion for this. They were supposed to share the burden, to make it easier for both of them. Too bad all this bond did was complicate things.

Once she figured out what they needed to do to save the future, that was it, she was done. She plopped on the bed and laid back, staring at the ceiling. Everything was so much easier when she was just stealing magick artifacts. Why did that stupid book have to call to her? What made her so special?

Cassie sat up and turned so her feet were on the bed

before laying down again. She just hoped she could sleep this time. The visions seemed to always come when she was sleeping. Sure, she'd gotten better about controlling them, but they still surprised her sometimes. Maybe if she did fall into one, it would take her to her past and she could finally see who her dad was. Since Sanir, the man who sort of raised her and her sister's father wasn't hers.

She pushed the thought away. Sleeping was the only thing she wanted right now. Going down memory lane seemed like it would be just as annoying as the Wolf downstairs.

Delete Created with Sketch.

The smell told her something was wrong, even before opening her eyes. It was like old dirty books. The kind bound in leather and written in ink made a century ago. She knew what was going on. The book had taken someplace, but where remained to be seen.

Cassie opened her eyes and she was standing between two large bookshelves. They were filled to the bursting with what looked like old weathered copies of any book you could want.

She stepped quietly down the walkway towards the opening as a tall broad shouldered man walked past, his head buried in a book. Cassie couldn't make out his face, but his hair was familiar. It was silver like hers and short, but full of wild curls. She could see the sides of his dark glasses, but not his face.

This had to be her father.

The book was showing her the one thing she wanted to know more than anything. She rushed towards him, but he turned away from her yelling to the distance something about a Sophia from Crimson river Clan.

Cassie didn't know what that meant, but she felt something tugging at her. "No, not yet," she whispered. "I just want to see his face." The invisible cord that linked her to the present tugged harder and she felt herself slipping. "No, not yet."

Before she could say anything else, she was slammed into her bed and her eyes shot open. She sat up and put her hand on her chest, it was so hard to breathe.

What the hell?

Cassie closed her eyes and filled her lungs with air. The only thing that would bring her out of this was deep breathes or at least she hoped it would. This was more intense than the other times she'd come back from a vision and she usually had Carik there to help her.

"You can do this, Cassie," she said to herself. Finally, your breathing slowed and she felt more normal. She grabbed the little notepad she'd put near the bed in case she had a random vision and wrote what she saw.

Now the real test was figuring out what it meant.

CHAPTER 3

CARIK

He pushed his way up the stairs and stopped on the other side of the door. Cassie wouldn't want him to just run in, but he'd felt the way she'd been pulled back. Every time she used it, he felt it or went in with her. That was part of the bond the book had with Carik's clan.

He put his hand on the doorknob and swallowed hard. Maybe he should just knock first. She might not even need him. "Cassie, are you okay?" He waited. Nothing.

Carik turned the knob and stepped in. She was sitting on her bed with a little notepad in her lap. Her shoulders were slumped and she seemed like she didn't even know he was standing there.

"Cassie," he said again, kneeling in front of her. "What happened?"

She finally met his gaze. "What?" She shook her head. "I'm fine."

"You don't seem fine," he said. "You know I can feel when you have a vision from that damn book."

"Yeah, that's not creepy," she said with a bite. Cassie just stared at him.

"I can't control it anymore than you can." He sighed. "What did you see?"

"I don't want to talk about it," she snapped.

"Fine," he said. "We'll train some more tonight but this time, we'll work with the book."

"You want me to connect to it again in the same day?"

"You have to. We both know finding out who starts this war we saw is the only way to stop it. The longer we wait, the harder it will be to stop," he said, standing from the bed and heading for the door. He turned back to her and crossed his arms. "You will get this. We just have to keep trying."

Maybe he was hoping deep down that they would see something good. Maybe things didn't have to end this way if the future can be changed. The only thing that mattered to him was she was safe and he would do anything to make sure that happened.

CHAPTER 4

CASSIE

The last thing she wanted was to deal with Carik or to do anything in the future with him, but she didn't have a choice. The best and fastest way to get him to leave her was mastering the visions from the book and finding out what the hell started this whole thing.

There were so many possible threats that could start this thing. The most obvious were Demons. The problem is they never were what they seemed. All the dealings she'd had with them were her reading between the lines to put things together. That was honestly part of the reason she stopped working with The Order of Fate.

The other obvious ones were the Vampires but honestly they were just another type of Demon. They became the one most people thought about when they thought of what would be running around in the dark.

Warlocks were not on anyone's radar which made her think they were more involved than any of the others, but Cassie had limited knowledge and workings with them. She knew they had power as Sanir had already shown her, but she didn't know how much they had and how willing they were to help a Demon.

"Are you ready to do this?" Carik stood at the bottom of the stairs watching Cassie. She still was captivated by his dark eyes and the way he carried himself. Carik definitely worked harder on his body this year than when he first met her. And it showed.

"No, but it doesn't seem like I have a choice," she said with bite.

"I don't want to be doing this either, but we have a responsibility," he said as she jumped off the last stair and headed for the door.

"Story of my life," she mumbled. Cassie looked up at the darkening sky. The day had gotten away from them here in the small town Carik lived in. Everything was so quiet and peaceful. It was a stark difference from the sounds of the city.

"We should go to the sacred site," he said, shaking her out of her thoughts.

"It's more powerful up there for sure," Cassie said. "Why didn't we try that last time?"

"I wasn't sure you were ready."

"Why wouldn't I be ready?" Cassie raised an eyebrow as she spoke.

"There's a lot of power up there, like you said, but it won't do anything but make it harder if you aren't ready for it." Carik walked past her and Cassie followed.

"I guess that makes sense." She didn't say anything further. She hated that he knew more than she did about this power she was stuck with. Why didn't he just tell her what to do and how it works? Was he trying to make it harder for her?

They stopped at the edge of the space. It looked the

same as it did when they first came here before everything happened. She took a deep breath. Before her sister died and came back. Before everything changed.

She could feel the power coming from the spirals of the rocks in front of them. Each one carried its own power, but there was something about the way they were laid out in the grass that vibrated differently. It was so buzzing from the little rocks and the ground under her feet. She knew the moment she stepped into the first circle, she was going to get all the power in that place. It whispered to her and hummed in every drop of energy in the air around her.

"Once we get to the center, we can pinpoint that same time you saw the girl before," Carik said, taking a step towards the center.

"Grace," Cassie said, taking a step in and adjusting to the hum in her feet and the rush of energy in her body.

"What?" Carik said.

"Her name. It's Grace," Cassie corrected. This girl was the only person that had ever seen her in one of her future visions. She was different, more powerful. Grace might just be the key to saving everyone and changing the future. But they had to find out who the hell she was first.

"Then this is the best way to do it. This place connects to your power and my pack's power. It's where the book is going to be the strongest," Carik said, glancing back at her.

"I know. I can feel it," Cassie said without elaborating. The power was so strong. Stronger than she'd felt before when they were here. It had to be because she was connecting to the power of the book more than ever before.

She stepped closer to the center and held herself together the best she could. If she let go at all, she was afraid she'd be taken to the future or the past and have no idea how to direct it. At least this time, Carik would be with her.

The center was marked with an old stone altar with overgrown grass all around it. The place hadn't been used since the Witches walked away from the Wolves several decades ago, or at least that's what Carik says. She didn't know much of the history of the Wolves and even her own history was shaded with what The Order taught. Normally that meant they were only getting half the story.

"Take a seat and we can see where the book decides to take us," Carik said, standing by the altar.

"You want me to sit on the altar?" Cassie cocked her head. "Sure, that seems like a great idea."

"It's the center of power here. You should be able to tap into it and find this Grace."

Cassie sighed and took a seat on the altar. The minute she touched it, power ran through her. Her breath caught and she felt Carik's eyes on her. Cassie slid her gaze to him and shrugged.

"It's a lot of power," she said quietly.

"That's the point, but do you think you can direct it?" His eyes locked on her and his brows scrunched together in concern.

"I don't know, but we have to try. The sooner we know, the better we'll all be," she kept her eyes on him and felt her heart break a little. She couldn't imagine a world where he wasn't with her, but he was the one who made it clear he didn't want to be with her. She had to remind herself of that every time she saw him.

"Close your eyes," he said, putting his hands on hers. She pushed the hurt in her heart away and focused on the future. The place where Grace was and what caused her present, and Cassie and everyone else's future.

She relaxed into the power and felt the electricity from the stone altar flow through her, every nerve in her body tingled and the energy raised around her. Cassie felt her cheeks get hot and took in a deep breath. The air smelled dirty and full of decay.

Her eyes slowly opened and she was standing in the middle of a city, but no one was around. The sun was burning into her skin and Carik was standing not far from her.

"Does any of this look familiar?" He asked and she shook her head.

"When I saw Grace, she was at the remains of The Order in New York." She glanced around them. While they were clearly in a city, this wasn't New York.

"This is further south," Carik said, taking in the buildings. They were tall and looked like they were part of a large city, but it was not the one she was aiming for. "Atlanta maybe."

"Why would we be in Atlanta?" She said,

He shook his head. "I don't know, but that's where we are."

Cassie walked past him and down the street. "I've never been here before. Where is everyone?"

"They probably left the city like they did in New York." He sighed. "Whatever happened is bigger than any of us ever thought."

"This isn't just for New York. This is global," Cassie said. The hope was always that this was isolated in just one area, but that clearly is not what happened. This was way larger and way scarier.

"We need to go back further. This isn't telling us anything," Carik said, turning towards her. He crossed his arms and shook his head. "The Vampires didn't do this much. There is no way."

"I thought after we got rid of the stone, it would change things, but it's still the same."

"We had to have missed something," he said.

"Or it wasn't what created this mess."

Cassie nodded. "Let me see what I can do." She closed her eyes and took a breath, letting the energy pass over her. She felt a tug of energy and let herself sink into it. She breathed deeper and felt herself fall into the energy. The air shifted around her before she felt grass under her hands.

Cassie opened her eyes and pushed herself up looking for Carik, but he was nowhere to be seen. The icy air pushed at her skin and she shivered. The sky was dark and in the distance she could hear thunder. The eery part was there was no birds in the air or sounds from the insects and she was in the middle of nowhere.

She stood still and held her breath for a moment, trying to put together where the hell she was. Movement to her left caught her attention. She snapped her head in that direction and waited, but nothing appeared. She sighed and shook her head. This was just her letting her fear get the best of her, but where the hell was Carik?

Cassie turned and ran right into a dark figure shadowed to her. She stepped back as it stood there staring at her with its shadowed face. She wasn't even sure there was a face in there at all.

"Stop putting your nose into something you can't stop," the figure growled. "You'll only get hurt."

"What do you care?" She snapped back.

"I don't but you will," it said.

And she was slammed back into her body. Her eyes flew open and Carik was watching her intently.

"Are you good?" He asked without taking his gaze from her.

Cassie nodded, not risking a word with the pain that was radiating through her body. The power that thing had was nothing she'd seen before and she'd seen a lot of things in her time with The Order of Fate. "We have to tell Lark," she managed after a few moments of sitting.

Carik nodded. "I'll get everything ready. We'll leave in the morning."

He didn't even ask her what she saw. It was clear in the way she woke up or he just didn't want to open up something that they couldn't finish. He was the one person that understood everything she was up against and the one person she knew would die to keep her safe. He already proved that when they fought Ami and he killed a Vampire no one had even gotten close to killing in a hundred years.

She watched that man walk away too many times, but this one was one of the hardest. All she wanted was to grab him and let him hold her, but he didn't want that. Not anymore. They had to protect the future or at least that was what he said. Maybe to comfort himself, but it stung every time.

"I'll get my things," Cassie said as she walked from the clearing back to the house. The tension was more than she could bear. "When this is over, what will you do?"

Carik glanced at her, his dark hair falling into his face. "I hadn't thought about it." He took a long breath. "Maybe get the pack back together."

"The pack?" Cassie knew this was once a place where the pack got together but she'd never taken the time to ask him about it. Shit, she didn't even know the history of his pack or his family.

"Yeah, it's been separated for a long time. Too long. We

need to get everyone back." He glanced at her and smiled. "If we can't stop this future you saw then we will be stronger together."

"In the future, I didn't see any wolves. This place was gone and everyone in it," Cassie thought about the memory and her blood went cold. The buildings burning, everything in this tiny town was gone to flame and war. There was nothing left here. If they stayed, they'd die too.

"Maybe that's why we need the pack strong." He forced a smile. "To protect this place and everyone in it."

Cassie didn't say anything and they finished the short walk to the house. She glanced up in time to see Kierin leaning on the edge of the huge southern porch. He raised his eyebrows at us.

"Find anything useful out?" He said indifferently.

Carik looked at him and then to Cassie but didn't answer.

"Why? Do you actually want to do something helpful?" Cassie quipped.

He smiled and she couldn't help but smile back. There was something about him that infuriated her, but also put her at ease. Carik grumbled as he passed by them, but didn't say anything.

"I'm always helpful," he said as he watched Carik go inside. "What's his problem?"

"Not sure, maybe you should ask him?" Cassie said as she made her way past him and into the old home herself. Everything in this place was old right down the pictures that lined the walls of the little entryway. She hadn't noticed them when she first came here with Carik or she just didn't want to. Knowing people was hard when she knew Demons or Vampires could kill her at any time. Especially now that she basically was the book that told the future.

She hurried up the stairs and into her room, grabbing only a few things. They weren't going to stay in the city long. She needed to tell Lark what was going on, but texting it wasn't going to be the way to do it. Maybe she could Face-time her and get a read on what was going on there first.

Cassie pulled her phone from the dresser and hit her sister's name.

"Hey," Lark said as she put the phone up where Cassie could actually see her. She was sitting in her office/ The one Cody used to run The Order of Fate when he was still alive to do it. Lark took it over once the Vampire stuff settled. At least they hoped it had.

When Cassie killed their leader, Ami, she stopped the secession of that particular Demon line. She just wished they were able to find the stone that caused the whole mess in the first place. So far no one had even seen it. That on its own was not a good thing.

"Hey, how are things going?" Cassie pushed only a little just to see where Lark's mind was at.

"It's going. Did you find anything out?"

Right to the point, that one. "I might have. I need to talk to you in person."

She nodded on the other side of the phone. "Okay, you know where to find me."

"Always," Cassie smarted off. "I'd be surprised if you left that building."

Lark laughed slightly. She looked tired and drained. Cassie knew she went through a lot not even a month ago. She'd died and come back to life. That had to be the worst kind of hangover you could get.

"I'll be there tomorrow," Cassie said without hesitation. "We can come up with a plan then. I'm pretty sure I know who or what causes the future to go bad."

Lark nodded. "See you then."

Cassie smiled before she hung up the phone and let out a sigh. Why were they always the ones that had to deal with this kind of thing? Couldn't someone else get the whole save the world seiche?

CHAPTER 5

CARIK

He didn't miss the way Kierin looked at Cassie as he passed them. That man had a thing for her long before Carik and Cassie were together. The first time he'd seen her in the living room of their home, he'd practically thrown himself at her. Now that she wasn't attached to anyone, he was going to lay it on thick and she was falling for it.

"Not my problem," he muttered to himself. It wasn't. They weren't together as he had to keep reminding himself when he wanted to reach over and touch her face or pull her into his arms and never let her go.

The pack would never approve, at least that was what Shirley, the woman who practically raised him when his father decided he didn't want anything to do with the pack, said.

Carik grabbed some items for the trip and shoved them into a duffle bag he had hiding in his closet. The best he could do was some dark jeans and a t- shirt he'd been given with his favorite band's logo on it.

What if she was right? What if he got the pack together

and it was completely destroyed because he brought them all back here? Carik sighed. No, he couldn't think like that. The past records showed they were stronger together. If there was some kind of Vampire apocalypse, they'd be safer if they were all in one place.

He grabbed his bag and pushed open his door where across the hall Cassie was doing the same. They locked eyes and he wanted to drop his bag and pull her into him. He wanted to tell her he was an idiot and they were better together.

Instead he flexed his jaw and walked down the stairs in front of her. "I'm ready when you are," he called behind him as he pushed through the front door and headed to his car.

CHAPTER 6

CASSIE

She watched him walk past her and shook her head.

Great, now I have to ride in a car with him for hours. This will be fun.

Cassie sighed as she made her way to the car. Without saying anything she opened the door and tossed it in her bag. The last thing she wanted was to go to New York now but maybe she'd find something else there. Something that might lead her to her father. Maybe there was something in Peggy's apartment that could help her. But first Lark and the future.

"So, you never told me what you saw," Carik said.

"Nope," she answered.

He glanced at her as he drove. "That bad?"

She didn't say anything. As it was Cassie wasn't sure she knew what happened. The figure never revealed itself to her, but just the presence of it felt like a Demon. It was possible Demons were the ones that started everything. They knew that after Ami was taken out of the picture, things could change, but how much none of them knew.

"I don't know why I couldn't go with you for that part

of your vision. It was like I was pushed out," Carik contin-ued. "Are you getting that powerful with the magick from the book?"

"I don't think it was me," she answered simply. "There was something else there. I'm not sure what it was." It did feel good to tell someone else about what she'd seen, but it also didn't help her to understand it anymore than she did before.

"Something else?" He shook his head. "When I studied the magick of the book before I found you, it never said anything about something else being able to tap in. "

"It didn't feel like anything I've felt before. It felt like this thing hijacked the vision completely."

"That's new," Carik said, watching the road as they got onto the highway. "I can check with some of the books the pack has when we get back."

"Yeah, that would be helpful," Cassie said before turning back to the thoughts of who her dad was. "I had a different vision before that."

"Of what?"

"I think it was my father," she said quietly.

"Really?" Carik said without looking her way.

"I don't understand it. He was in what looked like a library. His hair was silver like mine. He has to be related." Cassie glanced at him. A part of her was hoping he might know something but she didn't even know if she wanted to find out about her father. He'd never bothered to be a part of her life even before Sanir had him killed or at least that was what he said happened.

Carik glanced at her before turning his back to the road. "Can you go back to that and get more information?"

She watched him. Something in her was saying he knew more than he was saying, but she pushed it away. Carick wouldn't do that to her, right? "I don't know. I'm going to stop at Peggy's on the way back. She probably has something about him in her apartment."

"Are you sure you're ready to go back there after what happened?" Carik glanced at her and there was nothing but concern in his beautiful eyes. God, she loved that man. Why did he have to be so hell bent on keeping a barrier between them?

"I don't have a choice," she said quietly. He was right, a lot happened that night. A lot of that was her fault.

"Why don't you try to get some rest. We'll be back in the city in no time," Carik said with a bit of a smile.

She sighed. He was right, she probably should get some sleep. Cassie already had a hard time sleeping and these visions were only getting worse. They took so much out of her and even though she learned a lot more about how to control them, they weren't keeping her safe in the present. That was fully on her and Carik if he wanted to. And she was sure he did even if he didn't say it.

Cassie leaned back in the seat and closed her eyes, hoping for actual dreams to come.

CHAPTER 7

CARIK

He watched her for a moment as she relaxed and drifted off to sleep. He hated keeping secrets from her and when she found out, he knew he'd lose her. But it was for the best. The moment she knew her fathers side of the family was, she'd be honor bound to go there. That would only bring her heartache. And maybe him too.

She couldn't know what she was and none of the packs could know either. They would come for her and he didn't know if he could protect her from them. They didn't honor pack law and that would come at a price.

His phone buzzed and he pulled off the highway at the edge of the city. It was Shirley. She was the only other person besides himself that knew who Cassie really was and what she could do. Minus maybe his brother, but he wasn't going to announce it.

The text read:

Carik, the pack is calling a meeting. I'm trying to keep it from happening till you get back, but they want to discuss who will take over now that we are getting things back together. I need you here.

He sighed and put the phone back in his pocket. Managing pack business and what was going on with Cassie was harder than he thought. Shirley wanted him to be the next Alpha. He wanted to stay out of the limelight. It seemed like he was going to have to make a choice of his own if he wanted to keep Cassie safe from his pack and everyone else's.

That was all he knew for sure at the moment. She was going to be safe. No matter what sacrifices he had to make, even if it was his own heart. She was all that mattered to him.

"What happened?" Cassie said sitting up. "Why'd we stop?"

"Nothing. I just got a message from Shirley. The pack wants a meeting and she wants me there." He said indifferently.

"She wants you to be the Alpha," Cassie said for him.

He snapped his gaze to her. Carik never told her any of the pack business.

"I live in the same house. I hear things," she said with a shrug. "Are you going to do it?"

"It's a lot of work and with the vision bond we have, I don't know I'll have time," he said simply. "I never wanted to be an Alpha."

"Which is why you should be." She held his gaze and he felt himself losing his boundaries. He wanted nothing more than to pull her to him and claim her again and again. As if she knew what he was thinking, she leaned towards him, a smile on her face. His gaze slid to her lips. Those lips she'd used to do so many things to him.

"Why can't we?" She said simply.

"It has to be this way?" He said breathlessly.

"You know that's not true?" she moved closer and he swallowed hard before leaning away.

"Yes it does," he said. Carick didn't even believe what he was saying. How was she going to? "You should text your sister. We'll be there in half an hour."

Cassie sighed and pulled her phone out. "There. I sent her the text, but we should-"

"No," he growled. "I made my decision."

"I'm not one of your future pack members that just bows to you. This choice affects us both," She snapped.

God how he loved when she challenged him. "Exactly why it is going to be this way. Just business." He slammed the car into drive and took off into the city.

The last of the drive was quiet for once. He wasn't about to give her any reasons to talk to him again and she was clearly mad as hell. Better she was mad than dead. If he did become the Alpha and she was connected to him, she'd become a bigger target than she already was. He could hide her from the other packs as long as she didn't didn't dig too hard or at least the word didn't get out if she did dig up her father's legacy.

But that was a worry for another day. They pulled up to The Order of Fate headquarters. From the outside it looked like an old rustic building with nothing going on. Maybe someone from the historical society had made a big deal out of keeping it alive, but no evidence that anyone lived there. At least not from the outside.

"I'll wait in the car. Wolves aren't welcomed there and I don't want to be stared at," Carik said, putting the car in park.

"Fine," Cassie said with a shrug. She opened her door

and got out of the car. She glanced at him before shutting the door like she wanted to tell him more, but didn't.

He watched Cassie walk into the school and pulled his phone out of his pocket to text Shirley back.

Tell the pack I'll be back tomorrow. We can hold a meeting then and discuss who the new Alpha should be. Who's up for it?

It took only a minute or two for Shirley to text back.

You and Kierin.

CHAPTER 8
CASSIE

Cassie opened the door and walked inside without even thinking about it. The last time she was here, everything changed. She changed. But this also wasn't her home anymore and she knew that too.

"Cassie," a familiar voice screeched as she turned the corner towards her sister's office. She smiled when she saw the dark hair of someone familiar.

"Hey, Senora," she said simply.

"I knew you'd come back," she smiled and Cassie felt a little bad. She was younger than her and always looked for her when she was here, but Cassie didn't know a ton about her. All she knew was that Senora didn't have any active magick, but Cody insisted on her being here and learning. Probably another one of his secrets he never told them before he died.

"I'm not back," Cassie said. "I just need to see my sister."

"Oh Lark's in her office like always." Senora made a face

and sighed. "She comes out to talk to us about the dangers of Demon hunting from time to time. She said mockingly.

Cassie smiled. Of course Lark would be more protective than Cody was. Cody just sent Witches to kill things and never cared if they came back or not. That is unless they had a lot of power. Then he took an interest. She figured it was the years he ran the Order that made him so cold, but she didn't know for sure. "Thanks. I'll see you around."

"If you stay you will," Senora said with a smirk before walking away.

She made her way to the head office and knocked on the door. Lark didn't open it but she could hear her inside and opened the door. "Hey," she said with a smile and Lark looked up from the book she had open on her desk.

"Hey little sis," she said before closing the book in front of her. "I hope whatever you know is good. We need something bigger than the future is fucked."

"It's not much, but I think Demons are definitely behind this," Cassie said, taking a seat.

"We already figured that." Lark said, shaking her head.

"I mean some powerful ones. They somehow got inside my vision."

"How is that possible?" Lark said, seeming more interested now.

"I don't know. Something connected to the book maybe? Or it's a Demon that can travel into visions." Cassie shook her head. "It's big, Lark. There is a definite reason they want this chaos."

"Of course there is. It's always about chaos when it comes to Demons," Lark said with a sigh.

"Yeah, but this is different. This feels like someone who's playing the long game," Cassie said without thinking. She'd felt it when the creature spoke to her. This was something more powerful than they'd ever dealt with before. This was bigger than even the first Vampire.

"I'll talk to Pycot. He's got to know something if the Demons are gearing up for something."

"Do you think he'll even talk to you?" Cassie said, scrunching her nose. After what happened, she wasn't sure he'd want to stick his neck out for them again. I mean a Demon killing one of his own kind to protect a Witch was kind of a frowned upon thing in the Demon world.

"I can try," Lark said. "If not, there probably is someone here that knows something about Demons and can help out," she said sarcastically.

"Funny," Cassie said with a shake of her head. "Just be careful."

"I always am," Lark said.

Cassie watched her sister closely. There was something about her words that felt off. Something was different about her since she'd come back from the dead. She was almost darker in the way she viewed the world. Even if she didn't let that on. "Are you doing okay?"

"What do you mean?" Lark said sidestepping the question.

Cassie cocked her head at her. "You died or did you forget?"

"I don't like to think about it," she answered.

"But you know something changed, " Cassie pushed. Lark was different and she needed to admit it more than anyone.

"Nothing really. I just... Feel a little different." Lark shook her head. "It's nothing I can't handle."

"While you're also handling saving the world?" Cassie

put her hands on Larks. "You know I'm here. I know what it's like to have everything in your life change in a moment. You can talk to me."

"I know. " Lark said, grabbing her sister's hands and giving them a squeeze. "Aren't I the one that's supposed to be telling you this?" She gave a little laugh. "I'm the big sister after all."

"Even big sisters need support sometimes," Cassie said.

"I'll tell you when I'm ready," Lark said quietly.

"That's all I want." Cassie released her hands and leaned back in the chair. She hesitated, but maybe there was a book here that could help her or something in the history of the Order she could take with her. "I think I had a vision of my father."

Lark shot her gaze to her. "What?"

"Yeah, he had silver hair like me," Cassie shook her head. "I don't know where to look. I only know it was a library and they talked about something called the Moon River Clan. Do you know anything about it?"

Lark shook her head. "No, I've never heard of any clans in my research. But I was looking for things about Vampires. Maybe if you ask Blake. He's been here awhile and is always in the library. He'll know where to look if we have anything about clans."

"I'll stop there on the way out." Cassie glanced at the clock and made a face.

"What? You can't stay?"

"No, Carik has to be back soon. The pack is having a vote for the next Alpha. He needs to be there," Cassie said.

"It would be helpful for all of us if he was the Alpha." Lark said. "If we need any help from the Wolves with all this, he could be a good person on our side."

"Always thinking like a Witch from the Order," Cassie mocked.

"Someone has to," she said. "At least we can video chat."

"You could always leave someone else in charge and come down too," Cassie said with a smile.

"It takes like eight hours to get there."

"Not when Carik drives," Cassie said with a sigh.

"What happened with you to anyway?" Lark leaned back in her chair ready for that long story, Cassie was sure.

"He ended it. Said we needed to keep it professional for my safety," Cassie said and looked at the ceiling. It was better than looking at her sister who was sure to make it weird.

"That seems counter intuitive." She said. "It's not the Alpha thing is it?"

"Maybe," Casssie glanced at her and saw the real concern in her eyes. "I didn't want it. I just wanted him."

"One of us should be happy. I hope he changes his mind once he's Alpha," she said.

"You really think he's going to be the next Alpha?"

"I think if there is anyone that should be, it's him." Lark crossed her arms on her chest. There was the Lark Cassie knew her whole life.

"Me too," Cassie admitted. "He's the best option for them, and for us."

Cassie pushed the door to the library open and wandered in. She didn't know where to look or if this Blake person was here, but she was going to look as much as she could before they had to head home.

"Are you looking for something?" A male voice said from behind her. Cassie jumped and then turned to face him. Standing in front of her was a man about the same age. He crossed his arms and cocked his head and raised his dark eyebrows.

"Are you Blake?" Cassie asked before she told him anything.

"I am and you are?"

"I'm Lark's sister, Cassie." She glanced at the books behind her and then back to him. "I'm looking for information about clans."

"Clans?" He repeated. "The only books about Clans are in the wolf section."

"Wait, did you say Wolves?" Cassie eyed him as she spoke. If Wolves were clans, why didn't Carik tell her? He knows everything about the Wolves and him not telling her about this made her wonder.

"Yeah, they're the only creature that has clans as far as I know. Witches have Covens and so do Warlocks. Demons don't gather normally unless they are old school. They might actually have clans but I don't know a lot about their ways."

"Where's the Wolf section?"

"You don't know?" Blake laughed. "I figured Lark's sister would know where everything is."

"I've never looked up anything with Wolves," she said. He didn't say anything, but pointed to the left of her and along the back wall. "Thanks."

Cassie hurried to the section Blake pointed out. There were rows and rows of books lining the walls. This was going to take forever and she didn't have that kind of time. She glanced back to Blake who wasn't even looking her way before she said a spell she wasn't supposed to know, but good old Peggy taught her. When you want to find something, focus on the thing that makes it unique and say the spell. That was what she'd always said.

Cassie concentrated on the Moon River Pack and held out her hand. A book slid into her grip and she pulled it to her. Normally, they weren't allowed to take books out of The Order, but she hoped Lark would understand.

When Cassie turned the book to see the title, it was simply titled "The History of the Crimson Clan." She shook her head in confusion. That was not what she asked for, but it seemed that was what she was getting. Her phone vibrated in her pocket and she glanced at it.

Carik wanted to know when she was going to be ready. She typed back quickly and said she was coming, but a part of her was annoyed. She'd learned nothing about the man in her vision threatening everything or the Moon River Clan, but she had what she was going to get this time and maybe it would point her in one of the right directions. Plus Pycot was busy looking into the Demon side of things. With any luck they'd have something figured out before too long.

She slid the book under her jacket and walked back past Blake towards the door. "If you see Lark, tell her I'll catch up with her later."

"You didn't find what you were looking for?" Blake watched her with slight confusion.

"Not this time, but I'll be back before too long," she said as she hurried through the door into the hallway. It was already insanely late and it would take a miracle to get back before the pack had their vote. If he didn't make it in time, it would be her fault and Cassie wasn't sure she could live with that. After everything they'd been through already, she felt like she owed him.

If he'd never met her, he might have created a life without the book and without her. He might already have a family and a normal Wolf type life. But when they found each other, everything changed for him and she knew it. He was tied to her for the rest of his life and she to him even if neither one wanted to be.

She threw open the car door and jumped in. Carik glanced at her before starting the car and taking off.

"Did you find what you needed?" He asked as he pulled the car onto the interstate.

"I'm not sure. I'll find out more when I get a chance to read it," Cassie said, pulling the book out of her jacket and looking at it. The binding was older and the book looked like it had seen better days. Maybe it was just really old, she wasn't sure, but it was clear it was during the early days of The Order of Fate, which made it over a hundred years old.

"Did you know about the Order of Fate your whole life?" Cassie asked. She never thought to look into the Wolves when she was there and had no clue if they looked into The Order at all.

"I mean we knew about it, but we stayed away. Cody made it clear he didn't want the Wolves around," Carik said without looking at her.

"He ran it for a long time before he died, didn't he?"

"You would know that better than me, but as far as I knew it was decades," Carik said as he glanced at her. "When my pack separated, there was no one to turn to. We were alone."

"You didn't think about joining with the other packs?" Cassie watched him.

"That was a nonstarter," he said, his tone darker than before.

"But now it's not?"

"If I become alpha, we will reorganize and look out for our own. The pack is better that way," he said.

Cassie didn't say anything else, she just flipped through the book. It was written in dark red ink and she wondered if that was why it was called the Crimson Clan. She'd never heard of them, but she'd never heard of most of the packs. Lark was right though, they would all be better off with Carik as the pack Alpha. She just hoped they got there in time for him to make his case.

CHAPTER 9

CARIK

He didn't look at Cassie for the rest of the drive. The last thing he wanted was for her to ask any more questions about pack relations. He hated talking about that and it was so complicated even now. Everything was so fragile with the pack and with the ones around them. If they were smart, they would all band together and fight the Vampires, but most of the other clans didn't want that and the politics of it all would be worse than dealing with a rogue Vampire here and there.

Cassie was so curious about things and he didn't have answers he wanted to tell her. It was better she did not know from him and if she did figure it all out, at least he could be there to cushion the fall.

They pulled up to the house and Carik could see all the cars from the rest of the pack who'd come to vote for the next Alpha, but they were extremely late.

"You can't go in for this," He said and Cassie looked at him confused.

"Why?"

"Pack business and you're not a part of the pack," He said simply. "They won't want you there."

"So, where the hell am I supposed to go?" She said, shaking her head.

"You can hang out in the car I guess. It will give you time to read your book," He gestured at the little book she'd brought with her. "Once it's over someone will come out and get you."

Before she could object, he opened his door and stepped out of the car. He didn't have time to have a fight with her about his. If he was going to do this, he had to get inside and make his case. As soon as he opened the door, he knew something was off.

His brother was sitting on the couch with a beer and smiled at him. The rest of the room was filled with pack members laughing and having a good time.

"Hey big brother," He said with a smile. "I'm glad you could make it."

"What's going on here?" Carik said.

"What do you mean?" Kierin took a drink.

"The vote," Carik snapped. "We still have to vote for Alpha."

"Oh we already did that. You missed it," He said, standing and walking towards him. "Guess I'm the new Alpha now." He put his hand on his shoulder and leaned in closer. "You really should have waited to take Cassie back to New York."

"You planned this," Carik said.

Kierin just smiled. "Is that anyway to talk to your new Alpha?" He turned back to the others. "There are going to be some changes around here. Starting with who we work with. What has The Order of Fate ever done for us?"

"Nothing," A voice said from across the room. "Those fucking Witches should mind their own business."

"They have. You better not be talking about Cassie," Carik said with an edge.

"Now, now brother, Cassie is welcome here for as long as she wants to stay, but there will be no other Witches here as long as I'm Alpha and no alliances with them."

"Kierin, there are things at play you don't know about," Carik said.

"I could say the same to you," Kierin said before walking past him and through the door.

Carik followed him. "Where the hell are you going?"

"To tell Cassie the happy news. I'm sure she will be ecstatic to know I'm in charge now."

"You son of a bitch, you did this so you could sway Cassie into being with you, didn't you? You could give two shits about the pack," Carik said, shaking his head.

"I think you're projecting," Kierin said before opening the car door where Cassie was sitting. "Why the hell are you sitting out here?"

"Pack business," Cassie said, glancing at Carik confused.

"Oh well, that doesn't matter anymore." He held his hand out."I'm the Alpha now and you can go anywhere you want."

She pushed his hand away and stepped out of the car before looking at Carik and then back to Kierin. "Fantastic. I'm going to bed," she said before walking past both of them and into the house.

Carik couldn't help but snort laugh. "How did that work out for you?"

Keirin shrugged. "It will work out always does."

"Or you could just go back in there and say it was a

mistake and give Alpha to a leader that can really help our people."

Kierin snapped his gaze to Carik. "You think I can't take care of our people?" He shook his head. "You have no idea who I am. I was here when you were off with Cassie looking at the future. They had no one and I was here for them." He pointed to the house. "Where were you when the packs came calling trying to take our land?"

"Look, I get it. I wasn't here, but I am now," Carik said.

"For how long?"

"As long as it takes."

CHAPTER 10

CASSIE

She watched Carik walk into the house and shook her head. The fact she couldn't be a part of picking an alpha pissed her off, but she also wasn't sure she wanted to be in the middle of all this.

It didn't matter. She had bigger things and this really didn't involve her. Cassie just hoped whatever they decided, she wouldn't have to leave. Not yet. Not before she knew what the hell the Moon River Clan was and how her father might fit into it.

The book looked as though it was older than her mother would have been if she was still alive. The outside was worn and the pages were yellowed with age. She carefully turned each page looking through the words for anything that made sense.

Cassie noticed some of the pages talking about the different clans or packs as they were called now. This was clearly a Wolf thing she'd stumbled into. Then a thought crossed her mind and she shook her head. There was no way. She'd have known if her father was a part of a pack. He had to be like her, someone that was friendly with the pack but not a wolf. Her mother would have told her, right? I mean she didn't tell her about Sanir not being her father so anything is possible, but this?

The sound of a door slamming brought her out of her thoughts. Kierin came out first with Carik following behind him. His face was twisted and she knew the Alpha vote hadn't gone well. This was bad for her and them.

Cassie couldn't hear the conversation, but the way Carik looked said it all. She glanced through the passenger door at Kierin. He locked eyes with her and there was something behind them beyond the normal smart ass looks he usually gave her.

Fear.

He looked away before she could consider what was causing it. Cassie was so tired of everything going on here. Maybe this wasn't a safe place for her anymore. Maybe it was time to go back to the city and help Lark directly. At least then she wouldn't be in the middle of a pack issue where they shut her out anyway.

She threw open her door and stepped up to the two men. They both looked at her and she raised an eyebrow.

"Are you done?" She snapped.

"This doesn't concern you," Carik said, looking away.

"This concerns everyone," Kierin said.

"What is going on?" Cassie said, looking from Kierin to Carik.

"She deserves to know," Kierin snapped.

"Know what?" Cassie said, but something inside her told her she already knew. Everything she'd read matched up.

"Tell her Carik," Kierin almost snarled. "If you don't, I will."

Cassie slid her gaze from Kierin to Carik. He glanced at

the ground before locking eyes with her. The sadness was the first thing she noticed and she shook her head.

"You knew something and you didn't tell me," she almost whispered. "You knew this whole time and you didn't bother to tell me."

"It's not like that," he said.

"What is it?" Cassie snapped.

"You're father. We knew..." Carik said.

"Knew what?" Cassie answered. "Say it."

Carik hesitated. "You're father... he was one of us. He was a shifter."

And just like that, everything Cassie thought she knew about herself was gone.

CHAPTER II

CARIK

The moment he saw the pain in her eyes, his heart broke. This was the last thing he wanted to do to her, but he didn't want to add more pain. Maybe if she'd found out another way he wouldn't have had to tell her and none of this would be happening to him.

"Cassie, I'm sorry. I wanted to protect you," he said.

"You wanted to protect me?" She laughed and shook her head. "The more you try to protect me, the more you end up hurting me."

"I hoped you'd never have to know about any of that." He hesitated. "The way it feels to be rejected from a pack is so much worse than any lie."

"How do you know that would even happen? How do you know I wouldn't reject a pack first?"

"It's in your nature to belong. It's in all of ours," Carik said without taking his eyes from her.

"He's not wrong," Kierin added.

"You stay out of this," Cassie snapped, pointing her finger in his direction. "You are just as bad if not worse than he is."

Kierin threw his hands up in submission.

"I have the right to know about where I come from. You had no right to take that from me." She said, Her tone changed from angry to just sad and it broke Carik's heart.

He'd only done what he thought was right to protect her. She didn't know how violent that pack was and how they treated outsiders. Even if she was a descendant of a member of the pack. They wouldn't care and she would feel that deep rejection every shifter dreaded.

"Cassie, I'm sorry and you're right. I should have told you about what I knew when you asked."

"I wouldn't have had to run around looking for information if you'd simply told me what you knew from the beginning."

"I can tell you now," He said. A part of him didn't want to tell her all the things he knew about the Crimson Pack but he knew he had to earn her trust back and this was the best way to do that. Even if he couldn't tell her everything he wanted to.

He stopped when something caught his attention to the left. Along the tree line on the other side of the street something was either standing and watching them, or getting ready to attack. Either way they were out in the open and anything could get the jump on them. The way Kierin moved to the other side of Cassie let him know he'd sensed it too.

"Something is out there," he said, glancing around them.

"It hasn't attacked yet," Carik whispered. He glanced back at Cassie. "You can't stay out here. It could be something sent to kill you."

"I can handle myself," she snapped, clearly still mad at him.

"That's not the point. We're all vulnerable out here," Carik said, keeping his eyes in the direction of the tree line.

"It knows we see it," Kierin said.

"How do you know?" Cassie said after.

"It's moving," Kierin answered.

At that moment the figure stepped out of the shadows with slow steady movements. He moved in front of Cassie. If anything was there to hurt any of them, it would be her. She was the most valuable thing to the Pack and the Witches and whatever was trying to end the world would want her and the book stopped. The best way to do that was to kill her and silence the book.

Cassie gave him a hard shove, but his large frame didn't move. "I don't need you to protect me."

He ignored her and kept his stance in front of her. The creature crept closer and he readied himself for a fight. Until he saw him. He was unlike any Vampire he'd ever seen. His dark eyes flicked from Carik to Cassie and back to him.

"Walk away wolf," the Vampire said.

"Not a chance," Carik snapped back. Kierin stayed behind Cassie, but Carik could feel him staring at them both.

"That Witch is going to die. You know that," the Vampire continued, taking a step towards them.

"I can take care of myself, asshole," Cassie said with a bite.

The Vampire laughed, but stopped coming any closer. "You have power, but it's useless if you don't know how to use it."

"You aren't a normal Vampire," Cassie said. Carik looked at her and then back to the Vampire. "What are you?"

"The future," he answered.

Carik was getting tired of the back and forth. "I don't care what you are, get the fuck out of here before I tear you apart."

The Vampire laughed. "You would be dead before you shifted."

"Maybe, but Kierin would finish the job for me," Carik said with a slight smile. As much as he hated the way his brother looked at Cassie, he knew it was true. They would both die to see Cassie make it out of this alive.

The Vampire looked at Kierin and went back to Cassie. "Interesting." He said. "I'm delivering a message this time. Stop meddling and walk away, or die."

"I don't like when people tell me what to do," Cassie said.

"Death it is." He smiled and backed up into the shadows. "Don't say I didn't warn you."

CASSIE

"What the fuck was that?" Kierin asked before looking from Cassie to Carik.

Cassie didn't say anything. It all felt wrong and weird. She'd never seen a Vampire like that before. This was different. She felt the magick coming off of it. The way it looked at her like it knew what she was thinking. The thought made her shiver. How would she be able to beat something like that? She had to learn more about who she was before they used it against her and everyone she loved was dead. Because of her.

Now he was back somehow.

"Cassie, everything just got a whole lot worse," Carik said, still watching where Cody was not thirty seconds earlier.

"I know," she snapped. Everything was a mess. She didn't even have a chance to process finding out she was a fucking wolf before all hell broke loose. She had to warn Lark.

Cassie pulled her phone from her pocket and sent a quick text to her sister, but she got no answer. Maybe she was busy and would talk to her tomorrow or worse. Maybe She'd gotten the same visitor.

"We have to call the pack together," Carik said. He crossed his arms and watched Kierin.

"You want me to call the pack together over something we aren't a part of?" Kierin shook his head. "No."

"They can't fight this alone."

"They never asked for our help," Kierin snapped.

"No we didn't, but maybe we need it," Cassie said. "This just got a lot worse for everyone who isn't on their side. I don't even know who is or isn't my enemy right now."

Kierin shifted his gaze to her and waited. "You can make a choice to leave all of this behind. You're a wolf. You're one of us."

"I'm not one of you. I don't know what I am," Cassie said with a sigh. "I thought I knew who I was and what the future held for me. Everything changed the moment I found that goddamn book."

"Do you think it knew what you were?" Carik said.

Cassie glanced at him and shrugged. "I don't know." Everything she thought was true about herself was changing at a pace she didn't like. First her father wasn't even her father and now she was half shifter. What could she do with this?

"I need to know about my father. Who was he? What his pack is like. I need to or I'll never figure out who I am."

Carik stared at her but Kierin stepped in and put his hand on her shoulder.

"We can go if you want," he said while Carik eyed him.

"You know where they are?" Cassie asked. Maybe it was a bad idea. Maybe it was too soon after everything, but she had to know.

"Yes. But they won't be happy to see me," he said.

"You two are not going on your own," Carik said.

"They won't like seeing you either, Carik."

"It doesn't matter," Carik answered.

"What am I missing here?" Cassie glanced between the two men. Something was going on. Just what she needed. More drama.

"It's not important," Carik said. "Get some sleep. We'll need to leave early."

CHAPTER 13

KIERIN

He watched Cassie walk into the house even though she didn't want to before turning to Carik. "You know it's going to go bad, right?"

"You were the one that wanted to take her."

"I'm not talking about that. I mean you and Nakia." Kierin raised his eyebrows. "That's messy."

"It doesn't matter," Carik said and Kierin watched him for a moment. His brother wasn't someone who showed their emotions, just like their father. But right now it was written all over his face. He was scared and it wasn't because he was seeing his ex. It was because Cassie was going to see a part of him he didn't want to show her.

"If you want to stay, I can take her on my own. They won't bother me, being the Alpha and all."

"You really love rubbing that in my face, don't you?" Carik said with a slight smile.

"I can do it, you know," Kierin said. He didn't tell his brother all the things he did to keep this place running. How he helped the others in the town and when he started seeing Vampires popping up how he created the hunting parties keeping them at bay.

"I know, but you shouldn't have too."

"Says who? You?" Kierin shook his head. "You can't protect everyone."

"I don't want to." He sighed. "As much as you piss me off, you're still my brother."

"Maybe, but we both have parts to play now. You protect Cassie when she's connected to the book," He hesitated. "And me when she's surrounded by wolves."

"If she's going to be here, in this, she's going to need to understand pack politics," Carik said.

He was right. Neither of them bothered to prepare her for what could be as a wolf. It was a lot to add on to what she was dealing with already. "Has she mastered the book?"

"Not completely," Carik said. "She needs more time."

"That's one thing she isn't going to get."

CHAPTER 14

CASSIE

"How far is this place?" Cassie wasn't surprised Kierin was leaning on the car waiting for her. She was surprised Carik wasn't there too. "Where's Carik?"

"Change of plans. I'll take you." Kierin said, motioning to the car door. "We have a lot to talk about."

"A lot to talk about?" Cassie repeated and got into the car. "Like what?"

"Like history," Kierin said, closing the car door and putting the key in. "You need to know how things work in this world."

"Awesome, a history lesson," Cassie groaned.

"It's important. If you do or say the wrong thing, they won't hesitate to kill you." He sighed at the lack of reaction Cassie gave him. "They already will want to kill you because of who your father is and the other part of you."

"You mean the Witch thing," she smarted off.

"Yep," he said simply. "Moon river Pack is old school. They follow the old ways."

"That's what Carik said too."

"So, the first thing to know is if you aren't mated, you have no say."

Cassie stared at him and shook her head. "Wow, starting off with the most misogynist thing ever."

He shrugged. "I told you old school."

"So, I won't be able to ask questions?"

"You will be the lowest there, but lucky you, I'm an Alpha." He smiled and Cassie rolled her eyes. "They will answer anything you ask."

"Because of you," Cassie said. "That's why you're coming and Carik isn't."

"Something like that." Kierin didn't elaborate.

"What about my father?"

"What about him?"

"They have to know what happened to him," she said. "I know he died, but I don't know anything else."

"I don't know," he answered with a shrug.

I watched the road for a while as Kierin drove. It was nice not talking about the book or the future for once. While Cody's appearance complicated things, I at least was able to warn my sister. She assured me it would be okay and I should stay here with the packs. At least for now.

"One other thing you should know," Kierin said out of the blue. "Don't tell them about the book."

"Why?" Cassie had no intention of telling people she barely knew anything about that book anyway,

"We don't know what side they're on. They might use it against you."

"You mean used it against you," she corrected. "There's power in knowing the future. I know that much."

"Carik does care about you. He did what he thought was best," Kierin shifted.

"Everyone always does. But they fail to consider what I

want."

"What do you want?" He slid his gaze to her and she bit her lip. The way he looked at her with mischief in his eyes made her shift in her seat.

"To be normal. To just live a life without worrying what's going to happen and how I have to find a way to stop it."

"So, don't stop it. No one's forcing you to do anything."

"You mean just stop trying?" Cassie shook her head. "How could I live with myself if I did."

"How are you living right now?" He slowed the car and took an exit. "We're almost there. Are you ready?"

Cassie laughed slightly. "Ready to meet people who never wanted me in the first place? Sure why the hell not?"

The small gravel road stretched further than she'd hoped and dirt and grime kicked up behind them as he drove. They were nowhere near New York or even North Carolina. Somehow the time moved faster and they were further into the appellation mountains than she'd ever gone before.

A small town came into view and the energy became more aggressive than Cassie experienced before. Like it wasn't just her they didn't want around but anyone. Maybe that was part of the reason the town was so far from any kind of civilization. Or maybe she was just nervous.

"They look as inviting as ever," Kierin said as his gaze scanned the few people on the streets. They were glaring at them as they slowly drove through. "We have to stop at the Alpha's first as a sign of respect."

"Then what?"

"Then he'll tell us if we can speak to Wayo's family or what's left of them."

"I have a family?" It came out before she thought about

what that meant. There were people out there who knew she was alive and never wanted anything to do with her. Why would they now?

"Only a few. Your father had a sister. I'm not sure if she's still here," he said. "I didn't know them. I just put it together when you showed up."

"That night we met in the house?"

"The night I shifted in front of you and told you who I was, yes." He gave her a sly smile.

Cassie remembered it well. She was still learning how to control the book and he'd broken in to see the Witch causing the stir. Of course the moment he shifted from a Wolf to human everything was exposed. Wolves didn't seem to care about nakedness like humans did.

"Did you know I was part wolf?" Cassie wasn't sure she wanted to hear the answer.

"Yes, but we still don't know if you can shift."

Shifting, she forgot all about that little part of being part Wolf. "Does that happen?"

"What?"

"Wolves who can't shift?" She asked.

"No. We very rarely mate outside our packs or nearby ones," he answered. "Sometimes things happen though. There've been a few."

"They couldn't shift," Cassie finished on her own.

"It doesn't matter. You won't be staying in the Wolf world anyway. Once this future thing is fixed you'll leave and do whatever it is you do."

"Don't sound so happy about it," she teased.

"Who said I was happy about it?" He stopped the car and glanced at her. "Follow my lead. I promise you'll be safe."

"I'm not worried about me," Cassie said with a slight

smirk. Kerin was as unpredictable as they came and everything in her said he'd lose his shit if he thought anything would happen to her. That was a comforting thing at least.

He pulled the car further into the trees until a little white house came into view. It was run down and clearly had better days, but the thing that was interesting was the tingle in Cassie's fingers.

"What is that?" She asked, holding her hands in front of her. "I've never felt this before."

"I was afraid of that. It's what happens when you get close to your alpha. In this case, when you get close to Atlas," Kierin said, putting the car in park and glancing at her.

"I don't understand."

"You've been away from the pack your whole life. It's the Wolf waking up," He said.

Before she could ask him any questions, he was getting out of the car. She followed suit and he shook his head in her direction.

"I'm not sitting in this car waiting for you to have a conversation about me," she said with some bite.

"You promised you would follow my lead."

"I'm not too good at keeping promises." Cassie smiled and shut the car door. He just sighed and walked towards the little house. As they got closer she noticed the building may look like it was small, but it was because part of it was back behind and peaking through the hill. The part of the house she could see was just the beginning of it.

Kierin stopped in front of the screened in porch and raised his hand to knock when the inner door opened and a tall dark man with the most beautiful emerald eyes walked towards them.

"How dare you come here after what your pack did," He

yelled before giving the screen door and hard shove that made Kierin topple back a few feet.

"Atlas, it's nice to see you too," Kierin said.

"Get out of here before I call everyone here and I let them take you and you're little Witch out," Atlas spat. He glanced at Cassie and she couldn't fight the shrinking feeling she had. It was overwhelming and fucking annoying.

"You know who I am?" Cassie forced. Her voice came out quieter than she wanted, but at least she was able to speak.

"Yes, and you don't belong here," he snapped.

"She does and you know it," Kierin said.

"She's a Witch. Even if she has an ounce of her father's blood in her, she's still a Witch." Atlas looked at her and curled his lip in disgust. "She needs to leave before the Wolf activates. Or we'll be forced to reject her." He swung his gaze to Kierin. "Is that what you want?"

"I want to know where the rest of Wayo's family is," Kierin said without hesitation.

"He has no family. They denounced him when he fucked a dirty Witch." Atlas glanced at Cassie. "And made that thing."

"I can offer you a trade." Kierin said.

"I don't want anything from you or your pack. Besides you are nothing. Your pack has no Alpha," Atlas laughed.

"I'm the Alpha. I guess you didn't have that information," Kierin said with a smirk. "You tell me where her family is and let us speak to them and I'll owe you."

"The great Star Mountain Pack is going to owe us a favor?" He smiled at this. "Fine, but you must be gone by nightfall." He glanced at Cassie. "We don't need to deal with her."

CHAPTER 15
KIEIN

He held Atlas's gaze. This was probably a bad idea. God only knows what he's going to want from Kierin and his pack, but if it helped Cassie get some answers, it was worth it.

"Wayo's mother still lives by the creek on the other side of town. She can tell you where everyone else went, but that's the only one still here. After his betrayal, his sister couldn't stand the idea of being in the same pack." He stopped and glanced at Cassie. "She mated a wolf in the Moon Mountain Pack."

"That's clear out in Oregon," Kierin said.

"She's been gone a long time, but Moria's still here. Whatever it is you want to know about Wayo, she'll be able to tell you," He cocked his head to the side as he looked at Cassie closer. "You do look like him. Let's hope you can get what you need before you have a similar outcome."

"What outcome? Are you running me out of here?" Cassie said. Kierin watched as her stance faltered only a little. She was fighting the wolf. She was fighting the impulse to follow the alpha at all costs.

He laughed. "You have his attitude, that's for sure." Atlas took a step towards her and locked his green eyes to hers. He stepped closer until he was standing right in front of her, those eyes piercing into her soul. Kierin wanted to reach out. To help her, but he knew better. This was how she earned respect here. If he interfered, she'd never forgive him.

"I know who I am," Cassie said.

"Do you?" Atlas sighed. "You have no idea who you are, or what you are."

"That's why we're here," Kierin said.

"Mmmm, I sure hope that's the only reason." Atlas turned and opened the screen door to his little home before looking back to Cassie. "Don't bring your troubles here. We don't need them."

"Troubles?" She crossed her arms and kept her eyes on him.

"I hear things. We are not getting involved in a war."

"No one asked you too," Kierin said, watching the pair.

"You shouldn't either," Atlas looked right as Kierin. "Wolves survive. This isn't our fight."

"It's everyone's fight," Cassie said.

"And that's the kind of nonsense that got Wayo killed." Atlas stepped into the screened in porch and turned back to Cassie. "And it will get you killed if you're not careful."

CHAPTER 16

CASSIE

"So, I have a grandma." Cassie stared at the dash as she spoke. She knew she'd have some kind of family here, but she didn't know if she was ready to actually meet them. Especially if they were going to reject her. Maybe Carik had a point.

"She's going to know everything about Wayo, your father," Kierin said without looking at her.

"I know, but I think I rushed into this," she spat out.

"Cassie, I know this is fast. So much has changed in such a short time, but this is the only time you're going to get. Atlas isn't going to let me bring you back," Kierin glanced at her.

"I know. It's now or never," Cassie said it quietly. All these thoughts went through her head. *Would she like her? How would she react to seeing a child her son had with a Witch? Could she get through the betrayal her father did to their pack?*

"Cassie, I'll be right here with you," He said.

"Why? What makes you care so much about what happens to me?" Cassie let a laugh escape her lips. "If I remember right, you didn't want me around when we first met."

"You have no idea what I wanted when I first saw you." He let the words hang in the air. Cassie didn't ask any more questions. She had a feeling she wouldn't like the answers.

They made their way back through the little town and back towards the main road they drove in on. Cassie was happy Kierin knew where to go. If she went on her own like she originally planned, then she would be in a lot of trouble in a lot of ways. For once a man seemed to come through for her without asking for anything from her or trying to protect her.

Kierin pulled up to an older light blue home on the corner just on the other side of the town. Cassie felt her nerves building in her stomach and took a deep breath. This was it. She'd know everything about her father if her grandmother would be willing to talk to her.

"We'll go together," Kierin said. "But you can do that talking this time."

Cassie glanced at him and went back to the house. Her father had lived here once. It was the strangest feeling she'd ever had. Even with all her years of fighting against Demons and Vampires, this was the hardest thing she'd ever done. At least to this point.

Cassie stepped out of the car and walked to the door. Kierin stood beside her as she knocked and waited for one of her last living relatives to answer.

The door cracked open and she heard a sigh from the little crack before it opened all the way. A short chubby woman opened the door and looked Cassie up and down.

"I knew this would happen someday," she said. "I can't help you."

"Wait, I just want to know about my father," Cassie said

without hesitating. "I don't care about the Wolf stuff. I just want to know about him as a person."

The woman watched her for a moment. Her eyes fading from anger to sadness. "There's nothing to tell."

"Please. Just talk to me for a minute and I'll leave and never bother you again," Cassie pleaded. She had to tell her something. Cassie came so far and if she just learned one thing about her father, it would be worth it to her.

"Fine, one hour." The woman opened the door further and turned away from her. She walked through the house with Cassie trailing behind. She glanced at everything in the old home. All the pictures on the walls, the ugly couch that had to be from the 1980's. Everything. Her father had walked through here once. She felt it in her bones. His energy still lined everything like he'd never left. She wondered if the woman could feel it too.

"What do you want to know?" She said as though she was going through the motions and had no intention of letting her feel any of it.

"Who was he?" Cassie said as she took a seat on the couch.

"Wayo was quiet. He loved to read and work with books. He spent so much time in the little library we have here."

Cassie smiled as she thought about the vision she had with him walking down the halls with books lining every wall. It was his safe space.

"He didn't much like the way the pack operated," she said.

"What do you mean?"

"He wanted to change things. To make it less separated," she said. "The Alpha family didn't like that. They made it hard for him and Moira."

"They wanted to unite the packs," Kierin said.

"Yes, but the Alpha's didn't." She stopped and glanced through the window. "If they hear me say this, they'll expel me from the pack."

"I won't tell them anything," Cassie said, forcing a smile. After how Atlas had spoken to her, there was no love for him from her.

"He went to the city to speak with The Order. He wanted change, but needed them to back him in order to make it happen," she said.

"He was going to make a play for Alpha?" Kierin asked and shook his head. "Stupid bastard." Cassie gave him a look and he shrugged. "Being an Alpha is hard and taking one from another," he said shaking his head. "That's suicide."

"Unless you have a force behind you," she said.

"That's where he met my mother, isn't it?"

"I think so. I only met her once," she said. "The pack got wind of what he was doing and called a vote. He didn't have a chance."

"So, he was kicked out of the pack before he died?" Cassie asked. She never bothered to ask her mother about her father, mostly because she thought her and Lark had the same one, but now it made sense. They didn't want Cassie there because she was a threat. Just like her father was so long ago.

"Yes, but he never stopped trying to come back. At least not until he died," She said. "He was a good man." She shook her head. "He just wanted to help people. So many died in that war."

"War?" Cassie was confused. Her mother never told her about any war.

"The one between the packs."

"I thought that happened generations ago," Cassie said, looking from the woman to Kierin.

"Not for everyone," Kierin said. "My pack was torn apart well before the one that she's talking about."

"Do Wolves just go around destroying each other?" Cassie said with snark.

"Pack violence is well known. The wolf will not always stay quiet," the woman, her grandmother, said.

"That was my father's problem, wasn't it? He couldn't stay quiet and they killed him for it." Cassie regretted it the moment she said it. But something about it felt right. There was more to her father's death than just a Warlock with jealousy. This was deliberate. This was more than rage.

Cassie put her hand on her head as she felt the dizziness come on. *Not now.* She glanced at Kierin right before she felt herself falling.

Delete Created with Sketch.

The wet grass slapped her in the face and she opened her eyes. Her whole body was laying in the long grass but she had no idea where she was. Cassie sighed and pulled herself to her feet before glancing around her.

"Where did you pull us too?" A familiar voice said from behind her and she smiled. At least she wasn't here alone.

"Carik?" She said before looking back at him. He looked like he'd fallen straight out of bed. "Were you still sleeping?"

"What? No. I don't know." He rubbed his head. "Where are we?"

"I don't know," Cassie let whatever was going on with him go for now. "I was talking to my grandmother about my dad and then I ended up here."

"You're already there?" Carik shook his head. "I don't understand. Why are you there so early?"

She just looked at him with confusion. "It's the evening," she said.

"Fucking Kierin," he said. "I'm going to kill him."

"Do it later. We need to figure this out right now," Cassie snapped.

"It doesn't look like the future. Nothing's burning and there aren't any Vampires running around."

"No, but there's magick. I can feel it." Cassie let the draw of the magick guide her and followed it. Carik followed behind her but stayed far enough back he could shift if he needed to. Most of the time her visions were protective of her, but lately, things were changing.

She crested a hill and could see several people not far from them. She hurried closer until she saw him. Sanir was standing in front of her father. His sneer made him look even darker than when he'd try to kill her not long ago.

"Wayo, did you think a mangy mutt like you could take my wife from me?" Sanir shook his head, a dark strand of hair falling into his face. He pushed it back and he glanced towards Wayo.

"Sanir, we both know she won't love you like she does me. We're in love." Wayo said before locking eyes with Cassie.

She didn't understand the feelings running through her right away. Confusion that he was looking at her. He saw her and she knew it, but then there was something more bubbling up in her. Sadness.

The sadness of not knowing who he was or who she could have been if she knew him.

"You can't stop this, Cassie," Wayo said, watching her. "This is about more than us."

"How are you talking to me?" She asked.

"We're blood. Blood speaks to blood with the magick of

the book." He smiled slightly. "I always knew it would be you."

"Wait, you knew?" She looked back to Sanir who was standing still, frozen.

"There's a book in the pack library. It has what you're looking for," he said.

"I don't even know what I'm looking for," Cassie admitted.

"I hid it there for you. Cassie, Peggy told me all about who you'd be one day. She knew."

"You knew Peggy?" Cassie felt her whole world spinning. All the people she trusted were keeping everything from her. Peggy, her mother, even Carik.

She glanced behind her where Carik stood watching everything. He gave her a smile.

"Peggy saw me coming too," he joked. "I loved your mother. She was my everything."

"She's dead," Cassie said without thinking.

"She's with you every day," he said with a smile. "And so am I." He glanced to Sanir and back at Cassie. "You don't want to see this, Cassie. Go."

"Wait, did the wolves have anything to do with your death?" Cassie asked. A part of her wasn't sure she wanted to know, but she had to. She had to know who she could trust.

"Don't go down that road, kid. Stay with Carik and Kierin. They are your future now." He smiled. "I love you."

And just like that, she was shoved out of her own vision and laying face down on the carpet of her grandmother's house.

"Cassie, are you okay?" Kierin rushed to her and pulled her to him.

"I'm fine," she said.

"Vision?" He said.

"Yeah, but it's okay."

"No, it's not. You just told the entire pack you're connected to the book." He glanced at her grandmother. "Atlas is not going to let you go now."

Delete Created with Sketch.

"What do you mean Atlas isn't going to let me go?" Cassie felt a bit of panic rise up as she spoke. She came here to get information, not be stuck here because of her visions.

"Atlas is a man who likes power and you have it," Kierin said, helping her to her feet.

"If you hurry and go now, you might be able to beat him." Moira hurried to the door. "It looks clear for now."

"If I leave, I can't go to the library." She looked at Kierin. "I have too. My father left something for me there."

"We don't have time, Cassie." He pulled her with him as he headed for the door. "We have to leave, now."

Cassie shook her head. "What happens if I stay?"

"What?"

"What happens if I stay here?" Cassie stopped at the door and glanced between Kierin and Moira.

"You become part of the pack. You can't do anything without the permission of the Alpha," Moira said. "It's not a good life. Not here in this pack."

"We are not talking about this," Kierin said. He grabbed her arm and dragged her to the car. She tried to pull away but he was stronger. He opened the door and grabbed her shoulders. "Why do you make things so difficult?"

"What happened to not telling me what to do?" Cassie countered, but the fear behind his eyes caught her off guard. "What are you so afraid of?"

"Cassie, get in the car," he said calmly. It was chilling and she finally relented.

She pulled the door closed and glanced back to Moira who was watching the scene play out.

Kierin got in the car and closed the door, not even looking at Cassie. He pulled away and sped out of the little town. Cassie watched as everything she wanted to know faded away. She'd never know who she was and it was killing her.

"I'm sorry, but you can't stay there if they know what you are," Kierin said.

"Why?"

"Do you not realize how much power you have?" Kierin snickered. "Of course you don't."

"I get it, I'm a Witch and now I could be a Wolf. So what?" Cassie crossed her arms as she watched the sun start to fade.

"It's more than that," he snapped.

Cassie had never seen him like this before and it was unnerving for her. He was always laughing and joking. The worry on his face, this was different.

"What aren't you saying?" Cassie pushed.

He didn't look at her. "You are so blind to everything," he said quietly.

"Kerin, I just wanted to know about my family. My mother didn't tell me about him. I only know what I've found here." Cassie's chest stung with her words. Everything she wanted was now back there and she couldn't go back. Not if she was going to maintain a friendship with Kerin and probably Carik too. "You told me you'd be there for all of it."

"That was before you had that vision." He glanced at her. "Because you were already connecting to the pack, they all felt it. They all know what you are."

"How could they know? The only people that know

about the book are your pack."

"That's not true," Kerin said with a sigh. "It's bigger than just our pack. It could be any wolf chosen to go with the Witch."

"Then why wouldn't they realize I could do it? They know who my mother is and my father." She shook her head. "It doesn't make sense."

"It's complicated. I didn't even know everything until I became the alpha," he said.

"If there was so much danger, why would you let me come?"

He locked eyes with her for a moment. "Because I know what it's like to want to know who your father is. I wanted to give you that."

"You didn't expect me to have a vision," Cassie finished. She bit her lip. Cassie could tell him about what she saw in the vision. She could tell him about her father and the book he wanted her to find, but it wouldn't matter. Not now.

"Will this go away?"

"What?" Kerin asked. "The connection to the pack?" He turned to get on the highway. "When we get further, yes."

"So, that's it? I won't be able to tap into that side of me now?"

"Trust me, it's for the best."

CHAPTER 17

KIERIN

He drove without telling her more. If he told her everything he knew, her world would be more than turned upside down. Cassie needed to believe part of her family was who they said they were.

He understood what Carik did now better than ever before. He should have kept his mouth shut about her wolf side. Then she'd be back at their home. Even if she wasn't near him, she'd be safe.

He glanced at her as she leaned her head back in the seat and closed her eyes. She wasn't going to forgive him for a while, but at least she'd be alive and she would believe she could change things.

At least until he could show her who he was.

CHAPTER 18
CASSIE

She closed her eyes and thought about her father. When she saw him, he looked like everything she hoped he'd be. He was kind and wanted to help her, but she still was confused on how he could take control of a vision like that.

The only thing she'd seen so far that could do that was the dark thing that hunted her and they were a strong user of magick. They had to be a Demon. Not her father.

She fell deep into a void of darkness. It was nothing like her normal dreams.

The air was cold on her skin and her heart beat fast. *Where the hell am I?*

Cassie turned all around her, but nothing was there. In the distance she could hear snarling. The dark ground vibrated under her feet and she lost her balance, falling forward. When she hit the void, it changed to soft grass and dirt.

"Carik?" She glanced around her for him. When she had visions, he was almost always there. The one person she trusted to help her when everything else was falling apart, but no one answered.

"Weak," a voice snarled in the distance. "You think you have so much power, but you are weak."

"Who are you?" She called out as the scene around her shifted into dark trees with moonlight shining through the branches and falling on the grass and dirt.

"I'm what you're afraid of. You don't even realize how afraid you are."

"I'm not afraid of anything," she smarted off.

A laugh pushed through the air and made her breath catch. "You are afraid to fight. Afraid to lose. You're afraid of everything you are."

"I'm not," she shouted again. "What are you afraid of? You're the one still hiding in the shadows."

"You're not ready for me," the voice mocked. "So unprepared."

"I don't understand what's happening," Cassie admitted.

"Finally," the voice said. It almost sounded satisfied.. That pissed Cassie off a little.

"This isn't a vision, is it?"

"No," the voice answered. "This is something more."

"Tell me."

"No." The voice sounded almost angry before she finally saw it. Walking towards her was a beautiful white wolf. Its eyes looked familiar and not at the same time. Its white fur was dotted with a small bit of black on its legs, but the white matched her own hair.

"How?" Cassie managed.

"You triggered me when you went to your pack."

"Kerin said it would fade."

"I might, but you called me, loudly." The wolf sat in front of her.

"I didn't," Cassie said, shaking her head.

"You're so scared of who you are, but you don't even know who that is yet."

"And you do?" She was curious, but also concerned. What if this was all in her head and none of it meant anything real?

"I know you," the wolf said.

"My mother didn't tell me about any of this," Cassie said, sitting on the grass in front of the wolf.

"She didn't want to hurt you."

"That's not an excuse." Cassie sighed and shook her head. "I never got to know my father. I missed a part of myself I'll never get back."

"That part of you is right here," the wolf said, cocking its head at her. "But you have to be strong enough to accept it."

"What happens if I'm not?"

"Then I will wait until you are."

Delete Created with Sketch.

Her eyes flew open and she looked around her. They were still in the car on the way back. Cassie shifted in her seat and Kerin turned his head towards her.

"Are you okay?"

"Yeah," Cassie lied. "I just fell asleep."

"We're almost home."

They were almost home, almost to his home. Cassie felt more and more like there wasn't a place for her to call home. She could go back to the city, live with her sister at The Order, but that meant she'd be right back where everything started. If she was being honest with herself, that was probably where she belonged.

"Carik is going to be pissed you left without him," Cassie said.

Kerin glanced at her. "There was no reason for him to go. It would have caused more trouble."

"You keep saying that, but you never say why."

Kerin shook his head. "You're better off not knowing."

ing things from her. Things she needed to know to stay alive. "I'm so sick of everyone making choices for me."

"No one is making choices for you," Kerin said.

"Really, you made the choice for me to leave. You didn't give me a chance to say no."

"Did you want to stay there? You would be a slave to that pack."

"And?" Cassie snapped.

"They would use you for whatever Atlas wanted."

"And you aren't?"

Kerin snapped his head to her. "I've never used you for anything."

"Really? We both know that's not true." Cassie sighed. "From the moment you put the pack back together, you wanted to maintain control. That's why you didn't let Carik have it."

Kerin slammed on the brakes and pulled the car over. He put it in park and turned towards her anger all over his face. "I've never used your power for anything. I became the Alpha to protect my pack. If I had my way, you'd be on the way back to New York and never come back."

His words stung. "Then why haven't you?"

"Carik's in love with you," he answered.

"Sure he is. That's why he ended what we had," Cassie said.

"That's not why he ended it."

"I know, he wanted to protect me." Cassie crossed her arms. "I've already heard it."

"That's not why he did a goddamn thing," Kerin said before pulling the car back out and driving.

"You're an asshole."

"Every day of the week."

CHAPTER 19
CARIK

"What the fuck, Kierin?" He said flying out of the door and punching him square in the face the moment Kierin stepped out of the car.

He gave Carik a hard push even after his punch landed right where Carik wanted it too. Kierin wasn't walking away without explaining himself.

"Relax, Carik," he said before stepping past him. "She's fine."

"That's not the point. We were supposed to take her together."

"I was not going to deal with you and Atlas's nonsense on top of everything else," Kierin didn't stop walking until he got to the front door. "God, I forgot how hard you can hit."

"Both of you are getting on my nerves," Cassie said, stepping out of the car.

"Did you get what you needed?" Cassie countered.

He felt like he should have gone. It didn't matter what happened in the past with her. She needed him and he wasn't there. "I should have been there."

"It's over now. There are bigger things to worry about. Like finding out who walked into my vision and threatened me."

"What are you talking about?" Carik said. "You never told me that. When did it happen?"

"A while ago and no I didn't tell you because I knew you'd freak out," Cassie sighed. "Besides I was hoping I'd figure it out on my own."

"These are things you have to tell us," Carik snapped. He felt his anger and needed to keep her safe bubble up. He'd held it down so long so he wouldn't have to admit he still cared for her, but maybe that didn't matter. He was the only one that could keep her safe in her visions, but she'd have to let him.

"Look, Lark is looking into it. She is more equipped to figure it out than me unless he walks into my visions again," Cassie said.

"Okay, but still. We should be talking about this too." Carik glanced at Kierin. "Did anything happen while you were with them?"

"You mean did I change?" Cassie raised her eyebrow. "No."

He studied her for a moment. Something felt off. She was great at deflecting but the way she wouldn't meet his eyes told him something happened.

"Cassie, you can talk to me. I know things haven't been great between us since,"

"Since you dumped me because you need to keep me safe?" She glared at him and he cocked his head.

"I guess. If that is how you feel," he said.

"How I feel?" She laughed. "You are such an asshole." She stormed past him and he didn't say anything as she walked into the house.

"That's what happens when you can't make up your mind, brother," Kieren said, walking towards him.

He put out his hand and stopped him before he walked past Carik. "You're one to talk. I know why you are always so close to her. You think you have a chance."

"Please, you have no idea." Kierin looked at him and shook his head. "You have no clue what I've already given up to keep her safe and to help her get the answers she's looking for." He laughed slightly. "What have you done?"

CHAPTER 20

CASSIE

What a fucking asshole.

She almost slammed the door before remembering it wasn't Carik's house and wouldn't even hurt him if she broke the whole damn thing.

He wanted to tell her how she should react and be but couldn't even fess up to just walking away from something they could have been. She sat on her bed and laid back. Cassie stared at the ceiling for a bit before hearing Carik stomp up the stairs and throw open the door. She didn't bother looking at him. He'd probably just say that wasn't real either.

"You can be so insufferable sometimes," he spat.

"Takes one to know one," she said, not taking her eyes off the ceiling.

"So fucking childish and agonizing at the same time," he said, walking to the bed and standing over her.

Finally, she met his eyes and started sitting up. He met her halfway and held her there, not quite sitting up, but not laying down either. Thier faces inches apart.

"I would do anything to get you out of my head," he said. "But keeping you safe and alive is always there. I can't escape you."

"Then don't," she said. There was hope in her words. She liked to say she was over him and everything he'd put her through, but she knew she wasn't. He was the only person she'd ever loved and the only man that truly could understand what she was dealing with when it came to these visions.

"There are so many things you don't know," he said. His voice breathy.

"Tell me. No more secrets," she said, her hand pulling at his shirt.

"I can't," he said before his lips crashed into hers.

Cassie wanted to be mad, to push him away, but every part of her was screaming for him. Everything she told herself felt like a lie. There was only right now and only him and her.

She let him push her onto the bed as she pulled on his shirt. She needed it off of him. she needed to feel him, his skin, his heat.

Carik pulled her shirt off as he pinned her to the bed with his hands on either side of her head. She looked up at him and for the first time in a while she felt safe. He was her home. He was the only thing she trusted even if he didn't tell her everything. Even if he couldn't. It didn't matter anymore. All that mattered was him.

"Cassie, I'm sorry for everything," Carik said, but she didn't let him finish before she was kissing him with all the need she held inside for so long.

"I don't care," She said, pulling him down to her. His lips trailed her neck, kissing so gently as he trailed lower.

His teeth pulled at her bra strap. She arched her back as he pulled it down and off her body.

He traveled lower with his kisses until he was right there. His tongue flicked her clit and she moaned slightly. He did it again until she was bucking her hips for more. She threw her head back and let it wash over her. She let all the pleasure she was feeling outweigh all the hurt, all the lies and everything she thought she knew. All she wanted was this and him.

"Carik," she panted as he kissed her hard and pushed her to the bed. His cock rubbed against her folds and it threatened to undo her. "Please."

He smiled against her lips as she pleaded for him. She needed him inside her. She needed him to never leave.

His cock slid into her in one motion and she moaned loudly. He pushed against her and kissed her neck, holding her in place as his pace increased. She couldn't think or process anything. All she knew was she wanted him. No, she needed him. She needed the warmth of him inside her to take away all the pain of everything happening out there. Everything that threatened to take her life and turn it upside down.

His speed increased and she felt herself coming undone as he finished, his seed spilling inside her.

And everything in that moment was safe and happy. Cassie finally had everything she really wanted. She had him and she was never letting him go.

CHAPTER 21

KIERIN

The smashing of the door got his attention as people rushed past him. He ran to the door and Atlas pushed his way in.

"Where is she?" He looked from Kierin to Shirley and back to him. "You took one of ours, Alpha and we want her back."

"You only want her because of what she can do for you," Kierin countered.

"It's the right of our pack. You can't interfere." Atlas stepped closer to him. "You owe me a favor anyway."

"Cassie is off limits," He snarled.

"You really want to go to war over a woman?" Atlas watched him as he spoke.

"Do you?"

Atlas glanced at the others gathering around them.

"It looks as though they will do whatever I say," Kierin said with a smile. "We don't have to be friends, but we can find common ground here."

"There is none. Cassie belongs with her pack."

"Cassie is her own person and can choose what she

wants," Kierin said. Even as he said it, the lie rolled off his tongue. He had no intention of letting her go back there to these people who only wanted power and nothing else.

"Did she choose to leave?" Atlas watched him as he spoke. "I didn't think so."

"That's not your concern," Kierin quipped. He glanced at the others. "And you don't see her here so..."

"She's here someplace." He leaned in to Kierin and smiled as he spoke. "Tell me, did her wolf come yet?"

"It's time for you to leave."

"Not a chance. I think I'll stay and have a chat with our dear friend," Atlas said, stepping past him and taking a seat on the couch. He put his hands on the back and leaned into it like he owned the place.

"Have it your way." Kierin glanced at the other men in the pack and they stepped forward grabbing Atlas on either side to pull him out of the couch. He pushed at them and they stumbled back.

"You dare touch an Alpha?" He stood and stepped towards Kierin. "This is not how it's done in my territory. The Alpha's are the only ones that fight. You want to keep Cassie so badly, prove it."

"You want me to fight you?" Kierin said with a laugh.

"I see, you're afraid you'll lose." Atlas eyed him and Kierin sighed.

"I'm not afraid of losing to you," he said.

"Then accept the challenge and end this."

CHAPTER 22

CASSIE

She smiled and settled into his body. The way it fit around her and made her feel safe was one of the perks of him finally admitting he cared. His arm was draped over her body and his fingers settled on her stomach. Finally, things felt right. She wasn't worried about the man in her vision or any of the future stuff that seemed to plague her over and over again since she found that damned book.

She closed her eyes and felt herself falling. The sound of the fighting made her open her eyes. She was laying on the grass in front of the little house she was sleeping in right now. It was weird and eerie.

"What the fuck?" She said without thinking. The battle around her was loud and bodies were hitting the ground. To her surprise, Atlas was fighting right alongside them.She focused on what was going on and saw Kierin going head to head with some man. He pushed the man back and the man bared his teeth. Cassie shook her head. It wasn't a man at all, but a Vampire. She watched closer. They were all Vampires.

She hurried to Kierin and pulled at the Vampire as it swiped at Kierin's head. Cassie's hands went right through him. She couldn't do anything. All she could do was watch. Her gaze snapped to the other side of the fight towards the trees. A dark figure stood there watching everything play out and Cassie felt herself go cold.

It was the same man from her visions before. He was watching her, waiting to see what she would do.

"No, I won't let this happen," she said, shaking her head.

"What can you do?" The voice startled her at first. She wasn't used to the wolf.

"Help me," she said. Finally, she could see the white wolf standing near the door of the house. It watched her.

"I can't."

"You said you'd be there when I was ready. I'm ready," Cassie almost begged.

"No, you're not."

"I won't let them die," she said.

"You have to be willing to walk away from them." The wolf said, taking a step towards her. "Both of them and everything you have here."

Cassie shook her head. "I don't know if I can."

"Your pack needs you. You are the Wolf and Witch. You are the key to everything."

Cassie's eyes flew open and she felt herself gasp in gulps of air.

Carik tightened his grip around her. "What's wrong?"

"I don't know," she admitted.

Carik pulled her closer but sat up a little so she could see his face. "Was it a vision?"

"I saw Kierin and the others fighting Vampires. They were losing," Cassie said.

"When?"

"Soon. I don't know. The wolf was there," Cassie said.

"Your wolf?"

She nodded. Cassie knew this was not about him, but if he'd gone through this, then he might know what she can do. Cassie remembered the wolf's words and bit her lip. Should she tell him?

"It wants you to accept it," he said.

"Is that how it works?" Cassie said. "I just accept the wolf and then I am one?"

"Something like that," Carik said. He forced a smile. "It depends on the person."

"It said I wasn't ready. It said I would have to give up everything," Cassie said.

Carik pulled her to him. "You don't have to let it in. Eventually it will go away if you say no."

"But what about what I saw?"

"What about it?" Carik said. "We've dealt with Vampires before. We'll do it again."

Cassie didn't tell him she saw Kierin getting slashed and falling to the ground. She didn't have the heart. If this was going to happen, they had to win. Even if that meant she was never going to see them again and she had a nagging feeling she had to go back to her father's pack.

She had to save them even if it cost her everything.

CHAPTER 23
ATLAS

He waited for Kierin to respond, but just in case, he had the rest of the pack waiting to attack. While it wasn't his favorite thing to do, he'd do what he needed to in order to make sure the power Cassie held was in his hands.

They had no idea what she was, not really.

He'd made a promise and even if no one else could know, he would honor it and make sure Cassie became who she was supposed to be.

"Tick Tock, Kierin," Atlas pushed. "Your choices are limited. Give me Cassie, fight Alpha to Alpha or start a war you won't win."

"Fine, I'll fight you but I want it known, if I lose, Carik is my replacement," Kierin said before stepping past him and outside the home's door.

At least he was smart enough to protect his people. "Noted," Atlas said without hesitation. He had no desire to take this broken pack and the way Carik snubbed his offer years ago made him less interested in working with them all together.

He stepped outside and stood across from Kierin only glancing at his men to make sure they knew what to do if he lost. While Atlas had no doubt in his ability to win, he made sure the others knew Cassie was to come back to her pack. At least then she'd have a chance to claim her fate. Even if she didn't know what it was yet.

"Are you sure you want to do this?" Atlas gave him one more chance to just do what was right among packs. "Cassie is a Crimson Moon pack member. You don't want to deny her this future. Her wolf is calling to her. You know I can feel it."

"You just want her because she has access to the future. You'll use it for your own needs." Kierin shook his head. "You don't give a fuck about her."

"And you do?" Atlas pushed. There was something he wasn't telling him. "What makes her so special to you?"

"Carik loves her," he said simply. "She's family."

"It's more than that." Atlas studied him before he realized. "You're in love with her."

"Let's get this shit over with," Kierin snapped.

Atlas studied him a moment longer. "She's your mate."

CHAPTER 24

KIERIN

Kierin's gaze shot up to him. "She's not a wolf."

"She doesn't know," He said with a smile.

Kierin hated how much of this was easily readable by a man he was growing to hate so much. If Cassie never accepted the wolf, she would be free to be with Carik and he could at least have some form of peace knowing he didn't destroy her life anymore.

"Are we going to fight or have an uncomfortable chat?" Kierin asked, keeping his eyes on Atlas.

"This changes things," Atlas said. "We could be what we were supposed to be when Carik was given the chance to marry my daughter." He stepped forward. "We could be one pack like we were meant to be."

Kierin didn't let him finish before he punched him in the face, hard. "You mean you could be the Alpha and we could just fall in line." Kierin laughed. "I will never bow to you or your clan."

"That's a shame," Atlas said, rubbing his face. "I rather liked you."

A shrill scream tore through the air catching Kierin off

guard. He didn't recognize who it belonged to but there was something about it that chilled him. He watched as Atlas's eyes drifted in the direction and followed them. At the edge of the yard where his people were standing was one woman with dark hair and pale skin, a hand wrapped around her middle and someone behind her biting her neck.

Kierin glanced back at Atlas. "Vampires."

CHAPTER 25

CASSIE

The screams were the first thing she heard. Cassie looked at Carik who was already on his feet and dressed. "It's happening, isn't it?" She felt sick at the thought. If only she'd pushed a bit harder and they were able to warn Kierin.

"I don't know," Carik said.

"They're here for me," she said, pulling on her clothes.

Carik met her eyes and shook his head. "They will die before they touch you."

"You can't beat a bunch of Vampires."

"You said Atlas was there in your vision. If his pack is here, we have a chance," Carik said.

Cassie hurried to the door and Carik grabbed her. "You can't. If they kill you, then everything is lost. You are the key to the future."

"I have magick. It can help," she said. "Besides I used to hunt Demons, remember."

He gave her a look but she raised her eyebrows.

"You're not going to let this go are you?"

"Not a chance," She answered.

"Fine but stay close. We all need you to live," Carik said before they both ran down the stairs and through the door. Everything felt like slow motion. The Vampires were ripping at the others, pulling some of them apart, but others were able to shift in time to attack and keep themselves alive.

It was just like her vision.

Cassie pulled at her magick. She had pushed it down while living here since they didn't much like Witches, but now was the time to pull out everything she had. The energy pushed through her and she steadied herself. One wrong move and she'd hit a Wolf instead of a Vampire.

Lock on to the traits of the Vampires, The voice was gentle this time, like the wolf was finally there to help her for once. Vampires are dead, she just needed to aim at the dead and everyone else would be fine.

A scream and gurgling distracted her and she lost her hold on her magick. A stream of energy escaped her and knocked a nearby Vampire to the ground where a black wolf mauled it.

Try again. She licked her lips as Carik held a Vampire back who launched at her from the bottom of the porch. Cassie took a deep breath and closed her eyes. She grabbed the energy flowing through her. It was wild and strong but had no control. All this time she'd focused on controlling where the book took her and not where her magick lived.

It flickered with power. She was power. Cassie let it fill her until she couldn't hold it any longer. When she let go, she thought of the dead. The things that threatened to take the very lives of those she loved. She let the rage of everything she'd gone through push through her. The death of her mother, her father, the secrets. Everything.

Then there was silence.

Until there wasn't.

CHAPTER 26

KIERIN

The Vampire swiped at his face, missing him by inches. The last time he'd dealt with a Vampire was years ago. What did they want now?

"Kierin, they're here for Cassie," Atlas snapped. "If you really care about her, then we have a common enemy."

"Now is not the time for this," Kierin said as he narrowly avoided another slice at his face.

Atlas turned from Kierin and yelled at his pack. "Defend yourselves. For the pack."

Kierin couldn't help but roll his eyes. Of course he had to announce it. His pack was well aware they needed to protect themselves and Cassie. They didn't have to know why.

He punched at the Vampire and grabbed his head. They could survive a lot but getting their head ripped off was a no go. He wrapped his arm around the Vampire and yanked. Thank god for Wolf strength.

Kierin glanced around him at both Atlas's pack and his own falling to these blood suckers. But when he saw Cassie on the porch he about lost it. She shouldn't be out here.

They were here to kill her, to stop their only chance at saving the future or at least that was what Carik said every time he brought it up.

Kierin honestly didn't care about any of that. The future wasn't his concern. Cassie was. From the first moment he'd laid eyes on her before she knew what she was he'd loved her. That was the thing about mates. It came at the most inopportune time.

And now she was going to get herself killed.

He pushed through the fighting towards her and felt the energy in the air change. She was going to use magick. Kierin pulled a Vampire attacking a kid not older than seventeen off of him and stomped on his chest. He glanced at the kid, but before he could say anything the kid had taken a large knife and cut the Vampire's head clean off.

Kierin jumped up and ran as fast as he could to her. Carik was in front of her fending off any Vampires that realized she was out in the open and made a play for her.

But one slid past him and was too close to Cassie. Kierin jumped up the three steps of the porch past Carik and grabbed the Vampire.

This one was different from the others. He was stronger and his eyes held some form of human he'd never seen in a Vampire before. Kierin pushed at him and he hit the side of the house, but recovered quickly. The Vampire held up his hand and Kierin couldn't move. This Vampire had some kind of magick. How was that even possible?

"You have no idea what you're messing with, dog." The insult rolled off the Vampire's dark dry lips.

"You can't have her," Kierin said, he was fighting the hold with everything he had, but nothing would move.

"I already do," the Vampire said before running one fingernail across his neck and dropping him to the ground.

Kierin held his hands to his throat as the blood rushed out. He tried to breathe but he couldn't get air. All he could see was his brother standing over him, holding his neck to slow the bleeding.

"Kierin hang on," Carik said before everything went dark and quiet.

CHAPTER 27

CASSIE

"Kierin hold on," Carik said and Cassie opened her eyes. She glanced around her but every Vampire was a pile of ash on the ground. They were safe. They weren't on the ground dying.

"Cassie, it's Kierin," Carik said and brought her back to what was happening in front of her.

Kierin was laying on the ground beside her gasping for air. His throat was bleeding and his skin was going pale. She fell down to her knees and shook her head.

"No, no, no. He can't die." She glanced at Carik who was trying to hold it together. This was his brother and she couldn't let him go through losing everyone. "I..I think I can use magick to help him."

"There is no magick on earth that can save someone hurt this badly," Carik said. The panic was all over his face. He was going to lose his brother and she was going to have to watch it all play out in front of her.

We can save him. The voice caught her off guard. The wolf again. She closed her eyes and let herself connect to it.

"How?" she said into the darkness around her.

"It's time. Accept me and I can give you the power you need," the voice said.

She hesitated. A part of her wanted it. She could feel the power of her own magick and it would be magnified by the wolf, but the other part of her wanted to be normal. She wanted to forget all of this and just live a life with Carik.

"Choose."

"I can't let him die," she said. Everything screamed at her. What she was doing would change everything. It would change her future and the trajectory of her life, but it was the right thing to do. There was a pull in her that she couldn't explain. A pull that begged her not to let Kierin die.

"Say it," the voice said louder than before.

Cassie took a deep breath. "I accept you."

The slam of power was more than she could take. She felt herself double over in pain, her insides felt like they were being ripped in half. She let out a garbled scream and put her hands on Kierans.

"Save him," She said out loud before opening her eyes and watching the horrified look on Cariks face.

A stream of white power ripped through her. It circled around her wrist and Kieran's before snaking up to his throat. The wound leaking so much of his blood closing in front of her. The magick snaked its way towards Carik and wrapped around his wrist. His eyes softened and he looked down at Kierin. The power eased and Cassie caught her breath. Kirein's eyes opened and went from Carik to her. She only heard one word in her head from the Wolf as she leaned back and let the power settle.

Mates.

CHAPTER 28

"Did you do it?" A man standing in the shadows asked as the Vampire walked into the chapel. It was an odd place indeed for a Vampire to go, but when they called, he answered.

"I did," the Vampire said. "They saw my magick."

"That doesn't matter." the man veiled in shadow said.

"What is it about her that allows you to keep her alive?" The Vampire asked. He looked to his left to see a nun sitting quietly in the puh trying to keep herself together.

"That's my business," he snapped, leaning forward. The Vampire finally got a look at his silhouette. The cowboy hat and long duster gave him an odd look in a church of all places.

"What should I do now?" The Vampire asked. He was a servant for now but with the power this creature gave him, he'd be able to soon have some foothold in the world. Maybe he'd even get the Demons to listen to him.

"The sister. Make sure she stays in line." The shadowed man said.

"What do you plan to do to them?"

"I want them broken in every way." He said. "Make sure it happens."

to be continued............

ALSO BY TAVITA LANE

Moon River Mates

Blood Magick

Wolf Magick

The Order of Fate

Blood and Magick (Prequel)

Magick Thief

Night Magick

Destiny of Magick

Hunters Series

Burn

Hunt

Silver

Unforgiven